For Róisín, S.D.

To James and Phoenix
The most brilliant Humans
I know. S.H.

First published in 2016
by Faber and Faber Limited
Bloomsbury House
74-77 Great Russell Street
London WC1B 3DA

Designed by Faber and Faber
Printed and bound in the UK by
CPI Group (UK) Ltd, Croydon, CR0 4YY

Text © Swapna Haddow, 2016
Illustrations © Sheena Dempsey, 2016

The right of Swapna Haddow and Sheena Dempsey to be identified as
author and illustrator of this work respectively has been asserted in
accordance with Section 77 of the
Copyright, Designs and Patents Act 1988

A CIP record for this book is available from the British Library

ISBN/978-0-571-32330-2

2 4 6 8 10 9 7 5 3 1

DAVE

Pigeon's book on

How to Deal with Bad Cats and Keep (most of) Your Feathers

by Dave Pigeon

Typed by Skipper Pigeon on
Swapna Haddow's
old typewriter from the shed

Doodles by honorary pigeon
Sheena Dempsey

FABER & FABER

If you can read this, you obviously understand Pigeonese. You may carry on reading my book.

Signed: **Dave Pigeon**

If you're a cat and you've learnt Pigeonese (HA HA HA! As if a cat would be smart enough to learn Pigeonese . . .)

Wait.

If you are a cat and you are able to read this book, this must mean you have taken a pigeon hostage so that you can trick them into translating the Pigeonese words into 'Meow'. I demand you release the hostage pigeon immediately. This book contains TOP SECRET ideas that are NONE of a cat's business.

Dave Pigeon's
Pledge to All Pigeons

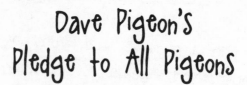

This is the true story of how I, Dave Pigeon, defeated Mean Cat, with the assistance of my trusty typer-upper, Skipper.

That's me, by the way.

I hope my success at getting revenge on one of the most deadliest cats of all time will help future generations of pigeons. Including you. Yes, you. No, not the pigeon behind you. YOU, reading this book right now.

Are you going to mention the—

Don't interrupt me, Skipper. I defeated Mean Cat. That's all anyone needs to know.

Dave is annoyed. He always fluffs his feathers when he's annoyed.

Now, where was I?

You were saying that you hoped your story would help all pigeons.

That's right. It will. That's why you must write down everything, Skipper. Starting right at the beginning.

The Beginning

Billions of years ago, before pigeons ever existed, the Universe was nothing . . .

I meant the beginning of this story, Skipper! Not the beginning of time.

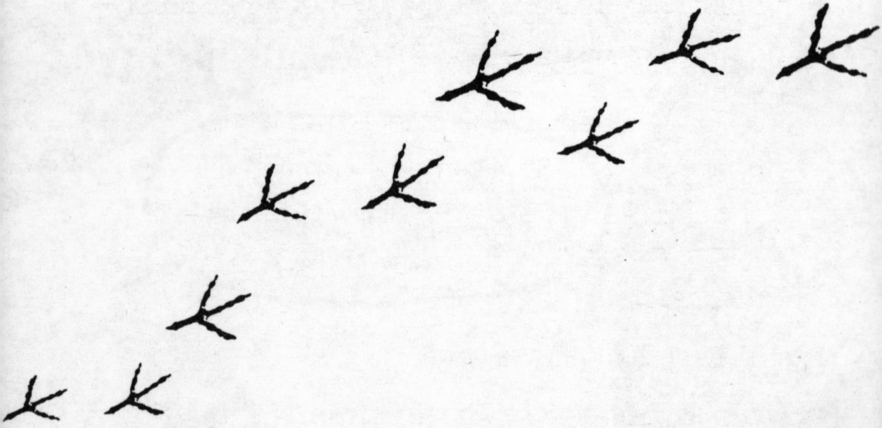

1
The Beginning of *This* Story Instead

Dave and me were on a routine croissant heist. It was something we'd done at least a hundred times before.

In fact, the first time I met Dave was on a croissant heist. Back then, Dave told me he had just won a Medal of the Brave which he wore all the time. (Though I

heard a rumour later it was just a bottle top that had got stuck to him with a piece of chewing gum when he got caught in a bin bag once).

Dave was swooping in from the opposite side of the pond when we both spotted a half-eaten croissant abandoned under a bench. We dived down, crashing towards the same gap between two planks of bench wood, and landed at the exact same time.

There we were, dangling upside down, stuck in the bench, when a huge goose grabbed our croissant and waddled off with it. A goose, for Bird's sake.

What I was about to say was – we never got our croissant back. We caught up to the goose just fine, but let me tell you something about geese. They are far bigger up close than when you see them in the distance. And they are very pecky. We were grateful to leave that fight with all our feathers.

Dave and I have been friends ever since.

Have you got to the bit where I almost lost my life?

Can you stop interrupting me?! I was just about to start that bit, but you keep ruining the story by giving things away!

Where was I? Ah, yes. The day we met Mean Cat. Our one hundredth croissant heist.

It was a bright, sunny morning, and me and Dave were starving. Peck-your-own-feathers-off starving. All we'd had for breakfast were the wet breadcrumbs a Little Human had already chewed and spat out, and a teeny-tiny piece of an iced bun we'd managed to steal from a duck.

That's when I spotted a Human Lady. We couldn't believe our luck. Everyone knows that Human Ladies like to carry around crusts with them. Dave said that's what their handbags were for.

Dave and I pattered over trying to look friendly and hungry.

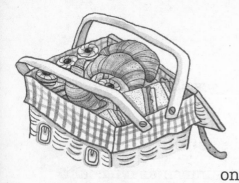

As predicted,
the Human Lady
popped the clasp
on her picnic basket.
There was more than just bread! Inside we
spied a feast of croissants, sandwiches and
biscuits. And they were the biscuits with
the jam in the middle. My favourites.

'Follow me,' I said, shuffling closer.

The Human Lady spotted us. 'Good
morning.'

We didn't say anything back because we
couldn't speak Human.

'Would you like some croissant?' she
said.

Of course we would.

She read our minds and tore off a piece

of golden-brown flaky pastry, throwing it towards us.

The sweet crumbs tumbled to our feet and we gobbled up as much as we could, filling our aching bellies. We inched closer to the basket, hoping to pinch a pastry or two for supper later.

'You two must be hungry,' the Human Lady said, throwing us broken bits of bread.

Dave cooed and hopped even closer to the basket. 'Come on,' he said, nodding at me.

I caught a whiff of something awful. 'What's that?'

'What?'

'That smell . . .'

'Sorry,' said Dave, fanning his bottom. 'I think it's that biryani from the bin I had last night.'

'Not *that* smell—'

The stink got stronger and stronger, burning my nostrils and stinging my eyes.

'Stop!' the Human Lady shouted. *'Stop!'*

A flash of ginger and white shot out from behind the basket. Sharp needles scratched my feathers.

The fiery stench of grass and wee meant only one thing. Cat.

Claws stung my back. I ran fast, took off and flapped for my life. Down below, I could see shiny strands of spit stretched across sharp fangs, as the orange ball of fur leapt after me, hungry for a bite.

'STOP!' The Human Lady grabbed her pet. 'Don't be such a mean cat.' She shoved the yowling beast down inside her basket.

Her eyes wide with shock, the Human Lady crawled across the grass and bent over the crumbs she'd thrown to us. I flew closer. There was Dave. My best friend was hurt. He was hurt bad. Full of croissant, he'd been too heavy to escape.

His left wing drooped, all twisted and ripped. The Human Lady gently lifted the limp feathers with her finger.

'Don't worry, pigeon, I'll fix you up,' she said.

The cat hissed from inside her wicker cage.

'You mean cat!' the Human Lady called

back. 'That wasn't very nice at all.'

She stroked my friend's broken feathers.
'I'll look after you.'

The Human Lady rummaged through
her bag, and pulled out a pile of napkins.
She carefully wrapped my friend in sheets
of tissue. When she had finished, he looked
like a roll of toilet paper with a beak poking
out at one end and two feet at the other.

I didn't tell him, but I heard Mean Cat laugh.

'We need to get out of here,' I whispered to Dave.

'No,' he said back.

'We can't stay here! Mean Cat will have us for lunch.'

My friend turned towards me, wincing in pain. His beady eyes narrowed and his nostrils flared.

'That cat will regret the day she broke my wing.'

'What are you going to do? Take her cat food?'

'Yuck,' Dave said, screwing up his beak. 'What would I do with disgusting cat food?'

He shook off the repulsive thought. 'No. We're going to teach that cat she can't mess with pigeons.'

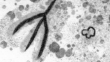

The Human Lady's Home

'Here we are,' the Human Lady said.

She carried Dave across a neatly cropped lawn, lined with yellow and purple flowers. Her front door was bright orange with a golden, sunflower-shaped knocker.

Mean Cat had skulked behind the Human Lady the entire walk back to her home. She hissed and spat at me as I

followed, careful to keep my distance from the menacing terror.

'What's going on?' a voice called out.

We all turned to watch a red-faced Little Human ride his scooter over the lawn towards us.

He spotted my injured friend straight away, and plonked his bottom down on the grass. He tugged off his left shoe and pulled off his sock, releasing smells of something similar to a cheese and pickle sandwich.

'Take this,' he said, waving the sweaty sock at the Human Lady. 'You can use it as a bandage.'

He then grabbed a bottle from the bag hanging on the front of his scooter and opened it, tipping some water into the lid.

22

Me and the Little Human watched as the Human Lady wrapped my friend up tightly in the damp sock, and fed him some water. Dave gulped down the drink and shrank back into the Human Lady's hands.

'Is he yours?' the Little Human asked.

'I think he is now.' The Human Lady smiled. 'I'm going to make sure he gets better.'

'What's his name?' the Little Human said, stroking my friend's head.

'I think I'll call him Dave,' replied the Human Lady.

'And who's that?'

They were both looking at me. The Little Human's arm stretched out so long that his plump finger almost brushed my beak.

'Oh, he's just another pigeon,' she said.

'What's his name?'

The Human Lady shrugged her shoulders. 'What do you think we should call him?'

'How about . . . Another Pigeon?'

'I'm sure we can do better than that!'

The Little Human stuck his face in

mine and stared hard. 'What about Prince Googlybrain Sizzlepants Ninja Mallet Face Wheely Shmeely Pancakeness Snotball Jelly?'

I shook my head at the Human Lady, praying she would say no.

'Perhaps something a little less snotbally?' the Human Lady said.

The Little Human tickled the feathers on my back with his podgy fingers. 'He smells a bit like the toilet after my Grandpa Skipper uses it.'

'Skipper is perfect!' the Human Lady said.

'I was thinking Toilet.'

'He's definitely a Skipper,' she said quickly.

The Little Human stroked my head one more time and shouted, 'Bye Skipper!' as he charged off, leaving track marks across the lawn and flower beds.

The Human Lady jiggled her hand in her bag, following the sound of her keys.

'Are you OK?' I called out to my friend.

'She wants you to call me Dave,' Dave replied, his voice weak.

'Are you OK, Dave?'

'Yes, but you need to keep that cat away from me,' he said.

The Human Lady opened the front

door to her house. Mean Cat pounced into the hallway. I flapped my wings hard against the front door.

'Does your buddy want to come in too?' the Human Lady said to Dave.

He nodded. Nodding means the same in both Human and Pigeonese.

I landed on her open palm and she carried us both through the house. Apart from the pong of cat, the Human Lady's home smelt wonderful. Every turn we took I caught the scent of bready treasures.

Dave's eyes were wide and a grin stretched across his tiny beak. We'd hit the jackpot. Moving in with the Human Lady meant we'd never have to go scrounging around the park for scraps of gravel-covered fruit roll-ups or lose our croissants to oversized geese ever again.

'You stay right there on your bed,' the Human Lady said to Mean Cat. 'Don't you hassle our new guests, otherwise there'll be no treats for you.'

Mean Cat growled from her cat bed. Then she must've remembered she hadn't tried to eat us in the last three and a half minutes, because she sprang at me, her claws glinting.

'Don't be mean!' the Human Lady said, shielding me and Dave. 'I'm very sorry about this,' she said to us. 'She's usually so friendly.'

I could describe Mean Cat as many things, but definitely not 'friendly'.

'Be good,' the Human Lady said to Mean Cat. 'These pigeons are our guests.'

She picked up Dave and tapped her shoulder for me to jump on. Mean Cat trailed behind as the Human Lady led us out of the back of the house, and towards a shed at the end of her garden.

She creaked open the lopsided wooden shed door, letting me fly in ahead, and laid Dave on a pile of paper by an old typewriter sitting on a tired, worn bench.

'You boys can stay here for as long as you want,' she said, dropping some bread by Dave.

Mean Cat snarled, staring at us.

'Out,' she ordered her cat, pointing the furball back towards the house.

The shed smelt of warm rain and newspapers. I pecked Dave free as he squirmed back and forth, unrolling himself from the Human Lady's napkin-bandaging and the smelly sock. He clambered to his feet, pulling me close.

'Can you believe this place?' he said, beaming. 'I'm sure I got a whiff of apple and blackberry pie back there.'

There was a tap at the shed window followed by two chirpity-chirps. A tiny canary pushed at the glass and jumped inside.

'You boys moving in?' she tweeted.

'Yes.' Dave nodded. 'We got here today.'

'I'm Tinkles.' She looked around the shed and whistled. 'You've done all right for yourselves.'

Tinkles was so small, she was somewhere between the size of a baby pigeon and a doughnut. She had a pointy pink beak and streaks of gold and white through her yellow feathers.

'Are you from around here?' I asked.

'I live next door.'

Dave looked out of the window, arching his neck. 'I can't see your shed.'

Tinkles chirped a laugh. 'Shed?' She shook her head. 'Not for me, thanks. I live in the house with the Human Man. I've got myself the full works. Private cage, my own bath and an endless supply of top-end bird seed.' She leaned in close. 'I've even got the brand new Super Swing. It has five speed settings and a cup holder.'

Dave grunted. 'We have biscuits and chocolate and pastries in *our* house.'

'Biscuits, you say?' Tinkles whistled again. 'Nice.' She hopped back up to the window ledge. 'It's a shame you don't live in the house then, isn't it?'

I headbutted the window back open. Tinkles fluttered out. 'Best be off, boys. I can't stay too long with that crazy cat around.'

She took off across the lawn, gliding over the fence back to her home.

Dave watched her go. He cocked his head to the side and looked at the Human

Lady's house. 'I don't know what a Super Swing is but I feel like we need one.' He waddled closer to me. 'We have to find a way to move into the Human Lady's house.'

'What about Mean Cat?' I asked.

'We're going to get rid of her.'

Skipper. If you don't mind, I'll do the chapter titles from now on.

What was wrong with naming chapter 2 'The Human Lady's Home'?

Booooooring!

3

The Plan that Involved Rain and which I, Dave Pigeon, Called 'The Rain Plan'

See? How much better is that chapter title now?

Fine. You do the chapter titles, but stop butting in because I can't remember where I was.

Dave's plan really was simple.

We were going to wait until it rained.

We would then drag Mean Cat's bed out of the house whilst she slept. The garden would flood with water from the torrential rain and we'd wave Mean Cat goodbye, as her beloved cat bed floated her away to the nearby river.

The river would grow larger and deeper as the rain got heavier. Mean Cat would wake up at this point, but there would be nowhere for her to go

because everyone knows cats are terrified of water and cannot swim.

Mean Cat would probably float for months, maybe even years, drifting far, far away.

Meanwhile me and Dave would move in with the Human Lady, who'd feed us croissants and biscuits every day.

'What about the Human Lady?' I asked, after Dave explained his plan. 'Won't she notice her cat is missing?'

'Of course not. She'll have us,' Dave said.

I peeked out of the window. Mean Cat was back in the Human house.

We waited for the rain.

4

~~The Plan that Involved Rain~~
~~and which I, Dave Pigeon,~~
~~Called 'The Rain Plan'~~

The Plan Where We Would Fly
Mean Cat Right out of the
House and Maybe She Would
Bump into a Few Windows but
We Wouldn't Feel Too
Bad about That and which
I, Dave Pigeon, Called
'The Flying Cat Plan'

and waited.

It didn't rain. In fact there was hardly a single cloud in the sky.

'We might need a different plan,' I said to Dave.

'Why?'

'Because it isn't raining.'

'And?'

'There isn't a cloud in the sky.'

'We don't need clouds, Skipper,' Dave said. 'We need rain.'

So we waited . . .

and waited . . .

Then fell asleep.

Then it was night time
so we kept sleeping.

Then it was morning and we woke up and it *still* hadn't rained, so we waited some more. And then waaaaaaaaited even more . . .

We were getting hungry, but Dave was determined to plot his revenge.

'Just in case it doesn't rain for a while,' he said, 'I think we might need a different plan.'

'I said that yesterday!'

'My plan is still for us to float Mean Cat away,' Dave said, ignoring me. He looked around the shed shelves. 'Get those for me, Skipper.' Dave nodded to a bag of colourful deflated balloons. 'I'll blow them up.'

The balloons were wedged under a toolbox. Dave was no help at all with his broken wing. I pulled and tugged at the plastic until the box toppled over, crashing to the floor and freeing the bag.

Dave picked up a blue balloon. He popped his beak in the opening and snorted.

The balloon lay still.

'I think you're meant to breathe into it,' I suggested.

'Quiet, Skipper,' Dave said, getting all huffy and fluffy. 'I know what I'm doing.'

Dave pushed forward into the balloon. His head stretched the blue until his beak pecked a hole in the side and popped out. Dave stood there, shaking his head, with a flat blue balloon hanging off his face. It was hilarious. More hilarious than the time he got trapped in a crow's nest by a crow that mistook him for a baby. He had

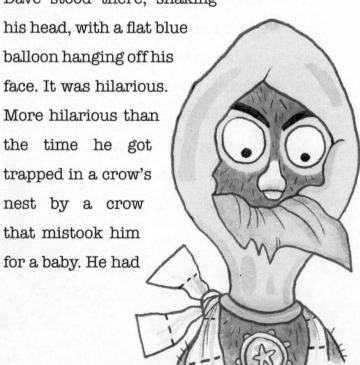

to eat slimy, greasy worms right out of her mouth to escape!

I had to bite my beak together to stop myself from laughing at Dave's head trapped in the balloon.

'Are you going to help me or what?' Dave squawked.

He kicked his head free from his balloon-face and rolled on to his back. 'That one was obviously a dud.'

He then tried to kick the dud balloon away, but it stuck to his foot.

OK, OK. It wasn't that funny. Let's move on.

Don't listen to him. Tee hee hee! It was hysterical.

Dave finally wriggled free from the balloon. 'You'll have to blow these up, Skipper.'

'Why me?'

'I can't do it. I already have a job. I have to make sure the plan is going to plan.'

'Can't we just use the pump?' I asked, pointing at a large gas canister on the floor.

Dave looked over. 'That's obviously what I meant when I said blow them up. Don't ask such catbrained questions, Skipper.'

I don't think he knew there was a pump.

It was very difficult attaching the balloons to the pump without making holes in them. And if you make a hole in a balloon, it won't blow up at all, which is so silly because it comes with a hole anyway. Of all the Human inventions, the balloon must be one of the daftest. How do they expect pigeons to blow them up?

'Do we really need balloons for this plan?' I asked Dave, throwing the tenth burst balloon to the floor. So far we'd only managed to get air into the green one, but we didn't know how to stop the air escaping. It whizzed and zoomed above our heads, flying off right out of the window before we could catch it.

'Yes,' Dave said. 'Otherwise it won't be the Flying Cat Plan.'

One of the red balloons seemed to be working. It grew and grew. I quickly pulled it off the pump spout with my beak, careful not to clamp too hard. It dragged me up and Dave caught hold of my foot to stop the balloon flying me out of the window. We slid the balloon neck under the side of the typewriter.

'Good job, Skipper. I'm sure that will do.'

'Are you sure a cat isn't too heavy for just one balloon?'

'Of course I'm sure,' said Dave. 'Cats aren't weighty. They are completely hollow on the inside on account of not

having a brain or anything else useful
under their fur.'

'How do we get the balloon on Mean Cat?'

'I have it all planned out,' Dave said,
nodding towards the shed door. 'Follow
me.'

The balloon kept tugging me up once we got outside. Dave clung on to my leg with his beak, and walked me and the balloon over to the Human Lady's house. We let it pull us up onto the window ledge, where we could watch Mean Cat.

She lay in her bed, pawing at what we hoped was a toy mouse. It was bright green, so it was either a toy mouse or a very ill mouse. Mean Cat's orange, furry paws smoothed over the mouse's body, and then she twizzled a claw into its ear.

'We're going to wait until Mean Cat falls asleep,' Dave whispered. 'Then you will go in and attach the balloon to her tail so she can float—'

'Why me?' I interrupted.

'Why you what?'

'Why do *I* have to go in there and attach the balloon?'

'Because you have two wings,' Dave said. 'You'll have to tie it to her tail.'

'But pigeons are rubbish at tying!'

'I know,' said Dave. 'Can you imagine how much more rubbish I'd be with only one wing?'

I looked through the window. The mouse had disappeared. Mean Cat was being very still.

'I'll keep the window open,' Dave continued. 'She'll float towards the window and right out of the house. She might bump into a few windows on the way out, but we won't feel too bad about that—'

'Dave!'

'What now, Skipper?'

'Look out!'

Mean Cat shot up at us. Orange fur and claws hurtled into the window. Dave stumbled back, toppling us off the ledge.

'Skipper!' Dave
yelled.

I dived down and grabbed Dave's
foot before he crashed onto the ground.
He flapped his wing fast, twisting around
and around in circles. We smashed into a
flowerpot, shattering it into pieces.

'Up to the ledge,' he shrieked.

Finally we dropped on to the wood, exhausted. Dave rolled over, laughing with relief. Through the window we could see Mean Cat on the floor. She yowled, nursing her bumped nose.

'What a catbrain!' Dave chortled. 'She jumped right into a window.'

'Sorry about the balloon,' I said. I'd let it go when I rescued Dave.

'Don't worry, Skipper. You saved my life.'

We watched the bright balloon shrink smaller and smaller in the sky.

'Besides,' Dave said, 'I have a better idea.'

5

~~The Plan that Involved Rain and which I, Dave Pigeon, Called 'The Rain Plan'~~

~~The Plan Where We Would Fly Mean Cat Right out of the House and Maybe She Would Bump into a Few Windows But We Wouldn't Feel Too Bad about That and which I, Dave Pigeon, Called 'The Flying Cat Plan'~~

The Plan Where We Used Our Hardest Stares to Scare Away Mean Cat and which I, Dave Pigeon, Called 'The Staring Plan'

We stared at Mean Cat.

6

~~The Plan that Involved Rain and which I, Dave Pigeon, Called 'The Rain Plan'~~

~~The Plan Where We Would Fly Mean Cat Right out of the House and Maybe She Would Bump into a Few Windows But We Wouldn't Feel Too Bad about That and which I, Dave Pigeon, Called 'The Flying Cat Plan'~~

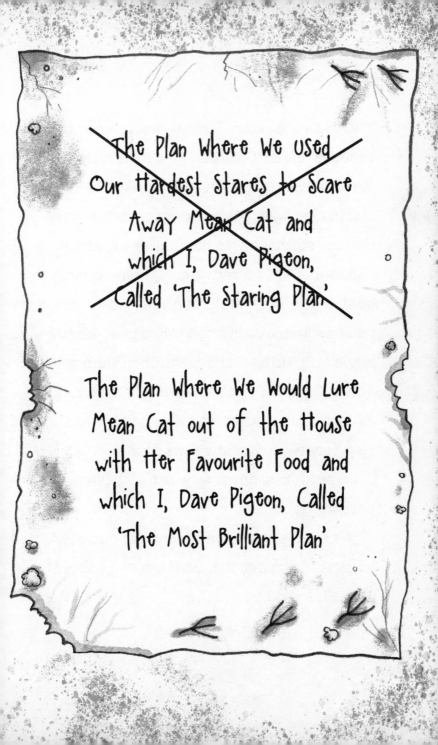

The Plan Where We used
Our Hardest Stares to Scare
Away Mean Cat and
which I, Dave Pigeon,
Called 'The Staring Plan'

The Plan Where We Would Lure
Mean Cat out of the House
with Her Favourite Food and
which I, Dave Pigeon, Called
'The Most Brilliant Plan'

The Staring Plan didn't work one bit because Mean Cat didn't even notice us. We'd been sitting on the window ledge staring for ages. My eyes were getting sore and my stomach was grumbling for lunch.

Mean Cat tossed her green mouse behind the sofa and then started to use one paw to play with the other paw, which is the only thing more catbrained than the Staring Plan. Or when Humans invented balloons. One thing was clear: she wasn't being scared away any time soon.

Dave looked down at Mean Cat playing her paw game.

'We need a way to lure Mean Cat outside,' he said. 'Once she's outside we can get rid of her for good.'

79

You asked, 'Did you type that?' and I said, 'yes.' Then you asked, 'That bit just now when I asked, "Did you type that?"' and I said, 'yes,' and then you said, 'Read me what you've just typed.'

Are we on the bit with 'The Most Brilliant Plan' yet?

Soon.

We sat on the window ledge, resting our feathers against the brick wall. The kitchen door swung open into the garden.

The Human Lady emerged from the house with a plate full of bread.

She spotted us up on the window ledge and made odd sounds at us, like she was flicking her tongue and sucking in on her teeth all at the same time. I'm not sure why the Humans do this to call animals to them. No animal in the world makes such a bizarre sound. Especially not pigeons.

Me and Dave flew down to join her anyway.

'Don't worry, little guys,' the Human Lady said. 'You're safe here.'

She held out a few crumbs in her hand. Dave climbed in and very gently pecked at the scraps of bread. The Human Lady offered her other hand to me. She was warm and smelt like buttery toast.

'There you go,' she said. 'Have some more.'

Dave hopped off her hand and gobbled up the crumbs that had tipped on to the floor. He edged towards the door to the house.

The Human Lady scooped him up and held him close. 'You can't go in there, Dave. That naughty cat will go for you.'

Dave buried his head in the sky-blue knitted wool of the Human Lady's cardigan.

'I wish I could have you in the house,' she said. She kissed him gently on his broken wing. 'But you'll be safer in the shed with your friend.'

She bundled us up together, nuzzling in and kissing us both on our heads as she carried us back towards the shed.

As we huddled together, surrounded by her long dark hair that smelt of loveliness and grapefruit, I turned to Dave. 'We have to find a way to get rid of that cat.'

'I've already thought of the most brilliant idea,' Dave said.

'Does it involve rain or balloons?' I asked as we settled back inside the shed.

'Nope.'

'Staring?'

'Nope.'

'What's the plan then?'

'We are going to lure Mean Cat out of the house,' said Dave. 'With cheese.'

'Cheese?!'

'It's a cat's favourite food, Skipper.'

'Are you sure? I don't think they even eat cheese.'

'Of course they do,' Dave said.

'I thought they ate mice,' I said. 'And

isn't it *mice* that like cheese?'

Dave sighed. 'Cats eat mice because mice eat cheese, so that means cats like cheese.'

'Because mice like cheese?'

'No,' Dave said, shaking his head at me. 'It's because mice eat so much cheese they taste like cheese.'

'Does that mean pigeons taste like biscuits and bread, because we eat lots of biscuits and bread?'

'Don't be such a catbrain, Skipper,' Dave grunted. 'Pigeons taste of chicken.'

I wasn't quite sure about Dave's plan, but the truth was we didn't have any other ideas.

'Where are we going to find cheese?' I asked.

Dave came close and tipped his head to one side. He put his one working wing up around my shoulder.

'You'll have to get it from the house,' Dave said.

'No.'

'Skipper. Do you want to get rid of Mean Cat?'

'Yes, but—'

'Do you want to live with the Human Lady with her wonderful warm hands?'

'Yes, but—'

'Then we need cheese.'

'Isn't there something else we can do?' I pleaded. 'If I go in the house, Mean Cat will eat me.'

'OK.'

Dave looked around the shed. He shuffled to the end of the bench and stuck his beak into a piece of paper, pulling it over towards me. He hopped back across the bench, his head bobbing as he looked up and down at the wall by the wonky door. Flitting forward, he hopped from one shelf to the next, until he landed on a wobbly wooden ledge at the far end of the wall. Then he began pecking through a glass jar full of odd bits.

'Dave, I wouldn't do that—'

He leaned over, dropping his head. I watched as his feet slipped out from under him. He tried to get a grip, desperately clawing at the shelf. His head jammed in the jar. The glass squished his face, making

his eyes bulge and his head look massive.
He looked like a pigeon alien.

'Mmpof marfing!' Dave yelped.

'Dave?' I managed to squawk between
bouts of hysterical laughter.

'Melph meeeeef!'

'Help me?'

Dave's giant glass head flopped up and
down in a nod. His one good wing flailed
uncontrollably as he staggered across the
shelf, his head bobbing back and forth.

I flew over and tried to grip
the slippery jar with my
feet as Dave pulled in the
opposite direction. He
flipped off the shelf and
crashed to the floor.

'I was trying to get this,' Dave said, carefully shaking the smashed glass off his feathers. He sifted through the broken jar bits with his jar-shaped head, and plucked out a short pencil stub.

'You're going to draw a cheese,' he said. 'Cats are dumb. Mean Cat will think it's real.'

It took about nine attempts to draw anything that even looked close to a cheese. Holding the tiniest stump of a pencil is quite hard when you have wings. The other problem was that one of the key things about a cheese is that it's yellow and we didn't have any yellow. We had a grey pencil and some black dust from a bag of charcoal near the door, and grey and black made not-yellow.

We had to stop for a nap because drawing cheese was one of the most exhausting things we had ever done.

'This isn't going to work,' I said, once Dave woke up.

We looked at my scrawls on the paper. I had spent ages drawing a cheese which

looked nothing like cheese. At best it looked like a wobbly pigeon egg.

'I think it looks fine,' Dave said.

It didn't.

So far, Dave's plans had been about as successful as a pigeon trying to ride a bike.

Dave *was* right about one thing. We needed to find a way to get Mean Cat out of the house.

We needed a plan that would work.

I watched Dave, slumped in a feathery heap as he muttered ideas to himself. The jagged edges of his torn wing stuck out, all twisted and broken.

I had a plan.

I knew Dave would say no. He'd say it was too dangerous.

I looked down at my own feathers. My wonderful wings. Dave would be right. My plan was risky.

But it was a plan that could work.

I shook off the sick feeling in my stomach. I knew what I had to do. There was only *one* way to trick Mean Cat out.

The one thing Mean Cat wanted to eat more than cheese was pigeon.

And that pigeon had to be me.

'I can get her out.' I kicked the drawing off the bench. 'I can be the bait.'

'No, Skipper,' Dave gasped.

7

The Plan Where We Would Lure Mean Cat out of the House with Her Favourite Food and which I, Dave Pigeon, Called 'The Most Brilliant Plan – Part 2'

Even though it was actually my plan that worked in the end!

~~The Rain Plan~~

~~The Flying Cat Plan~~

~~The Staring Plan~~

~~The Most Brilliant Plan~~

The Most Brilliant Plan – Part 2

'It's the only way,' I said. 'We need to get Mean Cat out of the house. We don't have any cheese but we do have me.'

I pulled Dave over to the window. My wings wouldn't stop trembling. I took a breath. 'Once she's out of the house, you need to jam the cat flap shut with the broken flowerpot so she can't get back in.'

'We still have the Rain Plan,' he suggested, gripping my shoulder with his good wing.

'The rain isn't coming,' I said.

Dave stared up at the clear blue sky.

He looked at me, his beak all straight and serious. 'Are you sure about this?'

I nodded.

'OK, Skipper. I believe in you.'

Dave removed his Medal of the Brave.
He peeled the tacky chewing gum from
his chest, and fixed the medal on to mine.
It gleamed in the sunlight.

'Once she's out, I'll lock the cat flap
from the inside and she'll be trapped in
the garden.'

Dave adjusted the medal on my chest.
'I'll let you in through the upstairs
window and we can come up with a plan
to get rid of her once and for all,' he
said. 'Our feathers will be the last pigeon
feathers she'll ever snatch, and *we* will

live with the nice Human Lady and eat biscuits all day.'

We headed back across the lawn. My throat was as dry as a cheese-mayo sandwich without the mayo. My stomach churned and twisted. Dave hid by the cat flap, ready to jump into the house and wedge it shut, his foot clutching a broken piece of flowerpot. He nodded at me and blinked twice: my signal to fly up to the window ledge.

As soon as Mean Cat spotted me she

sprang from her bed, baring her razor-sharp claws. She ran for the cat flap. She was coming outside to get me. As she pounced out, her nails clipped the edge of Dave's left foot.

'Ow,' Dave squawked, hopping on one foot and wedging the flap shut before he could jump into the house.

Mean Cat stopped.

Dave gulped, holding his good wing tight over his beak.

It was too late. She'd heard him. And he was trapped on the wrong side of the cat flap.

Mean Cat turned, dragging a single claw round on the paved patio, until she'd almost drawn a complete circle in the dark stone.

She blinked slowly as she spotted him quivering in the shadows of a tomato plant.

'Hissssss!'

'Help me!' Dave screamed.

I dived at my friend, grabbed him and soared away from Mean Cat as she leapt for Dave. Her hot breath blazed my bottom.

As I rocketed forward, she snarled, ready to pounce again.

'Faster, Skipper! Go FASTER!'

'*I am*,' I cried.

We spiralled forward as Dave flapped in circles, spinning us both towards the shed window. He knocked over a plastic pot of water by the window ledge. Mean Cat jumped at us at the same time as the pot plunged down, splashing water all over her. Her back arched. Wet ginger fur shot straight up all over her body. She howled, trembling and shaking off drops of water as she ran back to her precious cat flap – only to discover it was wedged shut.

She was trapped in the garden with no way to get back inside.

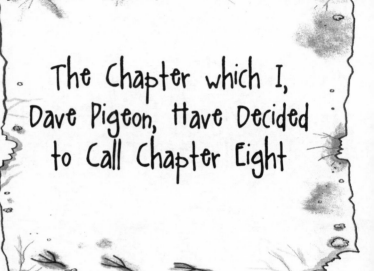

The Chapter which I, Dave Pigeon, Have Decided to Call Chapter Eight

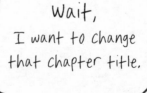

Wait, I want to change that chapter title.

8

The Chapter which I, Dave Pigeon, Have Decided to Call CHAPTER EIGHT

You know that's the same title, right?

Of course it isn't. The bit where it says 'CHAPTER EIGHT' looks much more chaptery.

It looks exactly the same.

Skipper, stop beak-flapping. There are pigeons out there waiting for this book, desperate to find out what happens next, and you are wasting time.

We were safely back in the shed. Mean Cat was pacing in front of the shed door. She was snarling and spitting and mad as a bagel-starved pigeon. Thanks to Dave's flowerpot lock she hadn't been able to get back into the Human Lady's house. And for the moment she couldn't get into the shed either.

'What was the plan once I lured her out?' I asked.

'I hadn't thought that far,' Dave said, panicked. 'I didn't think your plan would actually work.'

He marched up and down, flapping his good wing and jumping every time we heard Mean Cat yowl at the door.

'We need a cannon,' he screeched. 'We can launch her off into space!'

'We don't have a cannon.'

'You'll have to go inside the Human Lady's house and get one.'

'I'm not going out there with that cat on the loose!' I cried. 'Plus you don't even know if there is a cannon in the house.'

'Well, you'll have to go out there anyway,' Dave squeaked. 'I forgot to pick up our dinner from the garden.'

Out on the grass was a huge wedge of crusty, crumbly bread. And a very wet, angry cat circling it.

'I risked my life, and you couldn't even manage to think of a plan to get rid of Mean Cat—'

'I told you my cannon plan,' Dave butted in.

'— and, on top of that, you dropped the dinner?!' I continued.

'I've only got one wing, Skipper!'

He tottered off, his feathers at their huffiest fluffiest.

My stomach gurgled as I looked at the bread.

Dave's stomach growled back from the other side of the shed.

'Sorry,' he grumbled.

I ignored him.

Dave awkwardly flapped back across the shed and stood behind me. 'I said I'm sorry.'

He hopped in front of me. His eyes were

wide and teary. 'Friends?'

'Friends,' I sighed.

'I didn't mean to leave our dinner out there.'

'I know.'

'I promise I'll find a way to get rid of her,' he said. 'Cross my heart and hope to fly, stick a peanut in my eye.'

That doesn't make sense.

It makes more sense than sticking a peanut in your eye, I say. How do you even do that?

You get a peanut. And you stick it in your eye.

Dave's stomach was rumbling louder than thunder. I was sure Mean Cat could hear it outside in the garden.

'I can't get the bread,' I said.

'Of course you can, Skipper.'

Dave pulled over a plastic pot from the bench. 'Drop this on her. She didn't like it just now.'

'I think it was the water she didn't like.'

Dave climbed up to the window. He slowly head-butted it open, careful not to make a sound.

'I'll hold this open for you to get back in,' he whispered.

We were starving.

Outside on the lawn, the bread looked so yummy. Golden-brown on the outside and

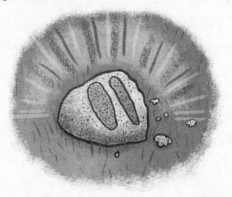

hard and stale on the inside. Perfect.

'Take the pot,' Dave said.

'What's the point?'

'Just take it!'

I grabbed the pot in my beak and squeezed out of the window. Mean Cat purred on the sun lounger as she dried herself against the cushions. I tiptoed as gently and as quietly as I could towards the bread. Flying would make too much noise and cast too many shadows.

I was about two beaks away from the bread when everything fell silent.

Too silent.

A long shadow inched over the bread, moving towards me like a dark cloud. I looked out of my right eye. There on the edge of the sun lounger was Mean Cat, leering, ready to attack.

There was only one thing for it. I beat my wings hard and flung my head to the right. The plastic pot careered towards Mean Cat.

Without looking back, I grabbed the bread and soared towards the shed window. Dave's eyes almost popped out of his head in terror. He grabbed me as I swooped in, slamming the window behind me.

We clung to each other, and watched through the glass as the pot smashed into the corner of the sun lounger, causing the top and bottom to snap shut. Mean Cat was catapulted through the air, high over the garden fence, until she was just a distant, meowing, ginger spot in the sky.

Dave grabbed me, jumping up and down. 'You did it! That sun lounger worked just like a cannon. I told you my plan was genius!'

I faced Dave and we screeched with laughter.

Mean Cat was GONE!

Did you think that was the end?
Of course it's not!

If you look at the
side of the book you'll see there are
loads more pages to read.

Take a break. Stretch your
wings. Go and look in a Human Lady's
handbag for some crusts to eat.
Once you're stuffed, come back and
read the rest of this book before
your friends do. Because they'll
probably tell you how it ends.

9
The Plan that I, Dave Pigeon, Came Up With WORKED.

But it worked a bit too well!

Dave grabbed my wings and swung me around and around as we whooped and cooed in celebration.

'She's gone, she's gone, Mean Cat is gone!' he sang. 'Iced buns for us and not for her, Mean Cat is goh-on.'

We galloped around the garden, jumping over the flowers and prancing through the weeds.

I lay back on the lawn. The grass dazzled

greener, the sky shone bluer and the washing line looked much lineier. Life was cat-free and felt birdrilliant!

'Shall we move into our new home?' Dave said, dragging me to my feet.

Me and Dave skipped across the backyard, chirping as we danced over to the cat flap. Dave bashed at the cat flap with his head and kicked away the broken shard of flowerpot.

'After you,' I said to Dave.

The cat flap rattled over us as we stepped into the Human Lady's house. It smelt like a breadcrumb paradise. A place where pigeons sipped strawberry fizzy pop all day through biscuit straws, and were fed pancakes and croissants covered in chocolate and peanut butter until they were stroked to sleep by warm Human hands.

We followed our beaks to the living room. It stank of Mean Cat so we didn't stay there long. The Human Lady must have been out because we couldn't hear her anywhere.

We headed back to the kitchen, searching

for the scrumptious biscuits
with the jam in the middle.

'What was that?' Dave said.

'What was what?'

'Did you hear that?'

We stopped and listened. In the distance
was the very faint call of a bird from the
backyard.

'That!' Dave said. 'Did you hear that?'

The coo came through a little louder this
time.

'It sounds like a pigeon.'

Then we heard another. Followed by
another. Then another. Then a squawk.

'What was *that*?' Dave asked.

He waddled to the table and jumped up
to look out of the window.

'Skipper!' Dave gasped.

The garden was heaving with pigeons. But not just pigeons. There were birds of all kinds. Big ones, small ones, parrot ones, grey ones, magpie ones, crow ones, duck ones and one that I didn't recognise at all but Dave said he was one hundred and three per cent sure was an ostrich.

'What are they doing here?' Dave hissed at me.

'I didn't invite them!'

'They might just want to say hello?'

'They want our Human house,' I said slowly. 'They want our food.'

'Let's throw out a biscuit. They can share it and leave.'

'Don't be such a catbrain, Dave,' I said,

terrified. 'They'll want to come in.'

Dave paced around in a tight circle. 'If we let them in they'll only invite everyone else, and everyone else will invite everyone else.' He rubbed his wing against his head. 'There'll be no food for us!'

'Why don't you talk to them?' I said. 'Tell them this is *our* Human house and they'll have to find their own.'

Dave headed out of the cat flap. He jumped up on to the handle of the watering can and struck the metal with his foot to get the birds' attention.

'Birdies and birdlemen,' he cooed. 'How can we help you today?'

A brown chaffinch with a blue cap

stepped forward. He threw his head back and tooted, 'Pip-pip-pip-pip-pip-pip-pip! Introducing Selentrus Vastanavius the Fifth. Leader of the Macaw Elite, Local Zoo Branch.'

A huge emerald-green-and-blue parrot, with a golden crown of crest feathers, leapt over the chaffinch and bowed. 'I am Selentrus Vastanavius the Fifth.'

He thrust his head high, and his yellow chest rippling, whistled into the sky.

Dave bowed back. 'I am Dave.'

Selentrus Vastanavius the Fifth nodded.
'I know.'

'That's because I told
him,' a voice tweeted
from behind the grand
parrot.

'Tinkles?' Dave said.

She hopped on to a moss-
covered paving slab. 'I hope you don't mind
me inviting a couple of friends over,' she
said. 'You did mention biscuits.'

'What about your top-end bird seed?'
Dave said, his eyes narrowing.

Tinkles shrugged. 'The truth is it tastes
like sawdust and chipmunk poop.'

Selentrus Vastanavius the Fifth fanned

out his huge wings and stepped back in front of Tinkles. 'Dave,' he crowed. 'We wanted to congratulate you on disposing of that cat.'

The garden filled with a chorus of hooting as the birds clapped their wings together, cheering for Dave.

'It was nothing,' Dave said to the crowd.

'It was everything,' the parrot said, bowing again. 'You showed true courage.'

'I suppose you're right,' said Dave, grinning.

'Now, if you wouldn't mind,' the parrot squawked. 'As Tinkles said, we are here to feast. Please would you open the door for us?'

Dave staggered back, almost falling into the watering can.

'We have wanted to dine here for many years, but that menace of a cat has always forbidden us,' Selentrus Vastanavius the Fifth went on. 'Now, thanks to you, we can enjoy the spoils of the Human's kitchen.'

The birds whooped and flapped their feathers harder.

'Unfortunately, the Human hasn't been to the shops yet so there is no food,' Dave stammered.

The birds straightened up. They stepped forward towards him. They weren't cheering any more.

'No food?' cawed Selentrus Vastanavius the Fifth. 'Not one morsel?'

'Not a scrap,' Dave lied.

The parrot glided across the lawn

towards Dave, his bright feathers skimming
the grass tips. He landed beak to beak with
Dave.

'Are you lying to us?'

'No?' Dave arched back, away from the
parrot.

'Well, I suppose you wouldn't mind if I took a gander for myself then, would you?' Selentrus Vastanavius the Fifth marched over to the cat flap.

'My friend is inside!' Dave shrieked. 'He's searching for the other cat.'

The parrot stopped. 'The other cat?' Selentrus Vastanavius the Fifth looked at Tinkles, who shrugged back at the confused parrot.

'There could be another one,' Dave nodded. 'Humans like to collect two of everything.'

'Are you sure?' Selentrus Vastanavius the Fifth asked.

'It's a Human thing. They love things in pairs,' Dave said quickly. 'Slippers, bicycle wheels, earrings, cups of tea—'

'Then why have I only ever seen one cat?'

'There might only be one cat,' Dave said. 'But do you want to chance going inside? What if there *were* two? Would you risk your lovely feathers?' Dave dipped his balding head towards the parrot. 'Besides, I'm sure the Human Lady will be back later with lots of food—'

'Quiet,' the parrot screeched, waving his long feathers. 'I need to think.'

'Just think of your feathers,' Dave reminded him, burrowing into his broken wing.

'Fine. We will return tonight,' Selentrus Vastanavius the Fifth said, eyeing Dave's featherless bottom. 'In the meantime,

you will conduct a
thorough search of
the house and ensure the
Human returns with food.'

He stretched out his bright
green wings and swooped
up into the sky, calling
the others up alongside
him.

'It will be quite
the   party

later, Dave,' he said, soaring ahead of the flock. 'You are a hero.'

I came out to join Dave as the last of the birds swept up and over the garden fence.

'What are we going to do?'

10
That Evening

Can I just say how annoying was that Selentrus Vastanavius the what's-His-Face? Who invites themself over for a party?

So annoying.

It would be like if we just turned up and then tried to kick someone out of their house so we could take all their food.

Isn't that what we did to Mean Cat?

Parrots are such catbrains. I'm so glad we're pigeons.

The sky grew darker as the evening sun disappeared into the night. The Human Lady still hadn't returned. Me and Dave sat on the porch by the cat flap, kicking tiny stones to each other.

'Dave, we can't let those birds in our house,' I said, breaking the silence.

Dave stared hard at the ground. 'I don't think we have much of a choice.' He got up and brushed off his feathers. 'Besides, it might be quite fun to have a party.

137

We are heroes after all.'

'You think this is a good idea?'

'Yes, Skipper,' Dave said. 'I've thought about it and now it makes sense. We *should* celebrate that we got rid of Mean Cat.'

'What about the Human Lady?' I asked. 'She might not like all these birds in her house.'

'When she comes back, we'll hide in the shed. That way she'll blame the other birds but still love us.'

The more Dave spoke about the party, the more convinced I became. We were probably the first birds in the history of birds ever to defeat a cat. We *were* heroes. These birds wanted to celebrate us. *With us.* Ever since that goose ran off with our

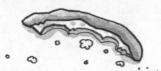

croissant, me and Dave had always felt a bit on the outside. It was nice to finally be respected for all the things we had done.

'We could throw the most epic party ever,' I said, jumping to my feet.

'Exactly!' Dave hooted. 'We'll be bird legends.'

We spent the next hour laying out the biscuits we weren't really that keen on and hiding the biscuits with jam in the middle in a fancy tin we found at the back of a cupboard. We pre-crunched the breadsticks and flattened the bread rolls just the way all birds like them. We even found some old pizza crusts in the bin to decorate the kitchen floor.

 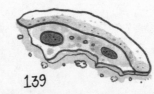

I felt jittery, excited and nervous. Dave was pacing, poking his head out of the cat flap every two minutes, checking for our guests.

'I see something,' he cooed, his eyes wide and twinkling.

We stepped out of the cat flap into the garden. There, high in the darkening sky, was a V-shape of birds soaring towards us. As they came closer we could make out Selentrus Vastanavius the Fifth, bright and green, leading hundreds of birds to our party. He swooped down and landed by the cat flap.

140

The blue-capped chaffinch stepped forward. 'Pip-pip-pip-pip-pip-pip-pip-pip! Introducing Selentrus Vastanavius the Fifth. Leader of the Macaw Elite, Local Zoo Branch.'

'Good evening, Dave,' Selentrus Vastanavius the Fifth said, stepping forwards. 'And Other Pigeon.'

'Actually it's Skipper,' I said back.

The garden filled with feathers and squawking as birds landed over the lawn, squeezing into any spare space, balancing on the washing line and pecking at the cushionless deckchair.

'There's a lot of you,' Dave said to Selentrus Vastanavius the Fifth.

'You know how it is,' the parrot laughed. 'I only told one friend but then they told a friend and, well . . .'

We looked across the lawn and saw hundreds upon hundreds of birds, all sparkly-eyed and ready to feast. Dave caught my gaze and shrugged.

'Shall we head in?' Selentrus Vastanavius the Fifth asked, edging towards the cat flap.

Dave nodded, gesturing the parrot in with his good wing.

As soon as Selentrus Vastanavius the Fifth had disappeared inside, the entire flock of birds in the garden charged the

cat flap. Tinkles stamped on both of my feet, her prickly nails scratching me as she raced inside. Feathers flew as Dave and I were shoved and pecked out of the way. Birds shrieked and trampled each other, tearing away at the cat flap, squeezing their feathered bodies through the small hole in the door. Dave's Medal of the Brave fell to the floor as we were swept aside by a heavy-set duck. A second duck stamped on the award, crushing it, as he squished himself through the crowds.

'What are you doing?' I shrieked at a crew of woodpeckers hammering at the doorframe high up.

'It's too slow through the cat flap,' a

small, stocky woodpecker called down. 'We're making a new way in.'

'Stop that!' I cried.

'No,' he crowed.

His two cronies flapped above me, blocking my way up.

'Skipper,' Dave screeched. 'Get down from there.'

I flew back to Dave, who had jumped into the watering can. We hid together. The metal rattled as we clung on to each other and watched the birds destroy the door.

The cat flap swung back, and out stepped Selentrus Vastanavius the Fifth.

'Enough!' he bellowed.

The woodpeckers stopped and cowered together. Even the stocky one flew away from the door and hovered by his friends.

Selentrus Vastanavius the Fifth held on to the handle of the watering can, offering us a wing as we clambered out. Dave's foot was stuck in the spout, but the parrot managed to wiggle the can to tip him out.

Selentrus Vastanavius the Fifth turned back to the woodpeckers, his eyes narrow and stern.

'Dave and Wallace—' he started.

'It's Skipper,' I interrupted.

'Whatever,' Selentrus Vastanavius the

Fifth said, waving his massive green wing in my face. 'As I was saying: these pigeons are heroes and have kindly invited us to eat all the food in this house—'

'You invited yourself,' I said, helping Dave to his feet.

'Like I said. Whatever.' The parrot raised his wing up to his face, shielding us from the woodpeckers, and spoke to us out of the side of his beak. 'Don't you want me to get these 'peckers to leave you alone?'

We nodded. A lot.

'As I was saying,' the parrot said. 'These pigeons are allowing us to eat here, so the least we can do is listen when they ask us not to peck at the door.'

The woodpeckers mumbled a 'Sorry,'

but as soon as Selentrus Vastanavius the Fifth had turned his back they stuck their long yucky tongues out at us.

The garden had cleared of birds, and the squawking had dulled to a din of chirping. Crackling biscuit wrappers drifted out from beneath the torn cat flap any time a bird went in or out.

Selentrus Vastanavius the Fifth waited until the last woodpecker was inside before he spread his green feathers wide, and pulled Dave and me towards him, under a wing each.

'That was a delightful spread you put on, Dave,' he said.

'You're very welcome.'

'The thing is,' the parrot continued, 'whilst those buns and breadcrumbs were quite tremendous, a few birds are a little disappointed not to have seen a better selection of biscuits.'

Dave pulled away and turned to face the parrot. 'Excuse me?'

'Don't take this the wrong way, old chum.' Selentrus Vastanavius the Fifth held his wings up. 'I'm only saying what everyone else is thinking.'

'And what is everyone else thinking?' I asked, my stomach twisting like there were a hundred fruit sours fizzing away inside it all at the same time. I thought of our favourite biscuits, hidden in that tin.

Selentrus Vastanavius the Fifth stopped. He tucked his wings in behind him and stuck his face in mine. 'Where are the good biscuits?'

'Wha-wha-what good biscuits?'

'You know which ones.' His eyes narrowed to slits. 'The biscuits with the jam in the middle.'

The cat flap flipped up and the racket of birds shrieking and cheering blasted out into the garden.

'We found them!' A red-and-blue macaw ducked out from under the flap. His beak glistened as the moonlight caught the sticky goo dribbling off it. Jam.

'No matter,' Selentrus Vastanavius the Fifth said, shoving us aside. 'It looks like my team have the biscuits now.'

I flew up to the kitchen window and sank down on the ledge, watching from the outside as Selentrus Vastanavius the Fifth ate his way through my biscuits. My special biscuits with the jam in the middle.

Birds pushed and shoved as they discovered where we'd hidden the croissants and crackers and iced buns. The fridge door hung off its hinges and cupboard doors were etched with claw marks and holes.

'They're never going to leave, are they?' I said to Dave as he collapsed next to me, gasping at the horror of the kitchen.

'No.'

'Won't the Human Lady get rid of them?'

'Yes.' He sighed. 'But they'll be back tomorrow.'

His eyes were wet as he juddered, trying to squash down his sobs.

'They might not,' I said, hopefully.

Dave shook his head. 'They'll take all

our food.' His neck sank into his shoulders. 'All of it.'

'Can't we do something?'

Dave didn't say anything. He was staring at a gold-framed picture sitting on

the kitchen worktop. There she was, our beloved Human Lady, snuggled on a sofa, her long hair swept over her shoulder as she smiled. She was cuddling her orange-and-white furry cat with teeth and claws as sharp as spikes. I followed Dave's gaze as he stared hard at the hairy terror.

'There is one way to make sure these birds stay away forever . . .' he said, softly.

He clambered to his feet and stuck his crumpled Medal of the Brave back on to his chest.

'Are you sure about this?'

Dave nodded his head once, his eyes squinting with determination.

'We need a plan. We need to get Mean Cat back!'

~~The Rain Plan~~
~~The Flying Cat Plan~~
~~The Staring Plan~~
~~The Most Brilliant Plan~~
~~The Most Brilliant Plan - Part 2~~

Watch out for more
Dave Pigeon
adventures,
Coming Soon!